W9-BAJ-867

THE HOUSE THAT JACK BUILT

JEANETTE WINTER

DIAL BOOKS FOR YOUNG READERS
NEW YORK

Published by Dial Books for Young Readers
A division of Penguin Putnam Inc.
345 Hudson Street
New York, New York 10014

Designed by Jeanette Winter and Atha Tehon
Printed in Hong Kong on acid-free paper

1 3 5 7 9 10 8 6 4 2

Library of Congress Cataloging in Publication Data
available upon request.

The artwork is rendered in acrylics.

This is Jack.

JACK carried lumber

from the mill,

to build his house

on top of the hill.

This is the **HOUSE**

that  built.

This is the **MALT**

that lay in the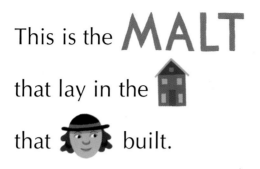

that  built.

This is the RAT

that ate the

that lay in the

that  built.

This is the CAT

that killed the

that ate the

that lay in the

that built.

This is the DOG

that worried the

that killed the

that ate the

that lay in the

that built.

This is the COW with the crumpled horn,

that tossed the

that worried the

that killed the

that ate the

that lay in the

that built.

This is the **MAIDEN** all forlorn,

that milked the with the crumpled horn,

that tossed the

that worried the

that killed the

that ate the

that lay in the

that built.

This is the **MAN** all tattered and torn,

that kissed the  all forlorn,

that milked the with the crumpled horn,

that tossed the

that worried the

that killed the

that ate the

that lay in the

that built.

This is the PRIEST all shaven and shorn,

that married the  all tattered and torn,

that kissed the all forlorn,

that milked the with the crumpled horn,

that tossed the

that worried the

that killed the

that ate the

that lay in the

that built.

This is the COCK that crowed in the morn,

that waked the  all shaven and shorn,

that married the all tattered and torn,

that kissed the all forlorn,

that milked the with the crumpled horn,

that tossed the

that worried the

that killed the

that ate the

that lay in the

that built.

This is the FARMER sowing his corn,

that kept the 🐓 that crowed in the morn,

that waked the 👨 all shaven and shorn,

that married the 👨 all tattered and torn,

that kissed the 👩 all forlorn,

that milked the 🐄 with the crumpled horn,

that tossed the 🐕

that worried the 🐈

that killed the 🐁

that ate the 🌾

that lay in the 🏠

that 👩 built.

This is the house

Jack built on a hill,

and if he's not gone,

he lives there still.